That
Old House

Sandra Clayton

Illustrated by Mark Payne

Rigby

Contents

Chapter One
The Day the Snail Came

The house had been empty for years, standing alone on the hill through rain and sun. Memories of families and friends clouded the dusty windows. Lonely, the house dozed the years through.

Until the day the snail came. He was looking for a home with a pantry full of leaves, out of the hot summer sun. He wasn't happy until he had left trails of shining silver across the walls.

The house stirred sleepily, then drifted back into its dreams.

The next day the rabbits turned up.

"Oh, I do like it under here!" exclaimed Mrs. Rabbit in the dark beneath the floor.

So she began to dig a burrow under the kitchen while Mr. Rabbit gathered food for her in the garden.

The house went on sleeping.

Soon a pair of mice came.

They went through the house
with mutterings and frowns. Mr.
Mouse measured the walls with a
fold-up ruler.

"Bit rough around the edges,"
he said.

"It'll do just fine," said Mrs.
Mouse hopefully.

"Hmm. Nice bit of real
estate," agreed Mr. Mouse, taking

a quick nibble of the wall, just to
be sure.

So in they moved, to be joined
by Grandma and Grandpa, Aunt
Edna, and brother Bill with his
wife and twelve children.

The skittering and chittering
reminded the house of holidays
and birthdays and excited children. The house shrugged and
settled down again.

Next came a deer hiding from hunters, a flock of wrens in need of garden seeds, a colony of bats in search of corners, and a stray cat who hissed and quarreled all night under the floors and on top of the roof.

The house felt troubled, but still it spun its dreams.

Chapter Two
All Kinds of Creatures

Sometimes there were quarrels. The cat and the rabbits fought over the new rabbit babies. The cat advanced, licking its lips. The rabbits retreated, growling and scared.

When the blue wrens flew down in a fluttering crowd, the cat sat down and pretended to wash itself.

But most of the time the animals were all good friends. They held parties, paid visits, and took care of each other's babies. They rattled through the garden jungle like marbles in a giant's palace.

But still the house felt empty enough to go on thinking and remembering, remembering and thinking.

Then along came the griffin. Some thought that a fabulous creature moving in was going too far.

"Mark my words," said the snail. "It's just the beginning."

"Oh, he's just TOO cute," cooed Mrs. Rabbit while the griffin blushed.

So the griffin stayed.

The house began to feel that it might be a good time to wake up.

Next came a unicorn with
gentle eyes and a story so sad it
would make a stone cry.

The unicorn gave the mouse
children and the rabbit babies

rides around the garden and acted as a judge for the others. The cat began to settle down.

The house shivered and rattled its windows, feeling like it was missing out by sleeping the new days through.

The dragon came next.

He was sweet and kind, though it's true he scorched a few things at first—the kitchen pantry, the wallpaper in the dining room, and the oak tree in the garden— but he soon fit in well.

Now that the nights were cooler, the animals gathered in the garden while the dragon started a cheery fire. The wrens and swallows sang, and the unicorn kept a sharp watch on the cat.

Sometimes the snail got there just as the others were turning in for the night.

Chapter Three
Wide Awake

The house was open-eyed now. It opened its doors and windows and let all its used dreams float away like last year's mist.

Now and then, the real estate agent drove up in her big, shiny car, mud splashing from the road. The animals would freeze, shrinking into the walls, the floors, or the eaves.

When the unicorn closed its sad eyes, nobody saw it. The griffin would creak and groan like an old weathervane on the roof.

"It's too creepy," the women would say.

"It's too old," the men would say.

The animals would breathe again as the big, muddy car jolted down the road.

But one day the real estate agent came with an older man and woman. The woman's eyes were so sad that the unicorn forgot to close its eyes and looked right at her.

"Oh, Sam," she cried, "isn't that a..." Then she turned away from the wall and rubbed her eyes.

"What do you think?" asked the agent, patting the wall. "There's still life in the old house, hey?"

The house shook with anger and dropped a load of plaster onto the agent's head. Backing up, the agent slipped on the snail's trail and landed right in a pile of garbage.

"I like it," said the woman.

"Me, too," said Sam. "But it's big for us, Della, and far from town."

"Yes," agreed Della. "It could be lonely since there's just the two of us."

Chapter Four
Sold!

The animals and the house felt uneasy after the agent's visit. The cat fought. The mice quarreled. The bats beat their wings. The snail talked about needing to be alone.

The unicorn was too busy thinking about the lady's sad eyes to keep the others in order.

To make matters worse, the house kept shaking and groaning. Just when the mice had settled their differences, the house scratched itself and sent one mouse flying into another. "I was better off without all of you," grumbled the house.

Then the man and the woman came back. This time they rattled up in an old, battered car stuffed with boxes and cases.

The animals froze.

Sam and Della smiled and hummed as they unpacked the car and carried in box after box.

THEY HAD BOUGHT THE OLD HOUSE!

Chapter Five
How Long?

The animals made themselves small while Sam swept floors and Della cleaned cabinets. But how long could the animals keep it up?

"How long?" creaked the griffin, turning in the breeze.

"How long?" groaned the house, shaking on its stumps.

Suddenly, the unicorn opened its eyes. It looked at Della and Della looked back.

"Sam," she said, "there's a unicorn here."

"So there is," agreed Sam, as he struggled to carry in a book-shelf. "Give me a hand, pal."

So the unicorn helped Sam.

And suddenly the house was alive with the scattering and chattering of the mice, the bats, the blue wrens (the swallows had left for the winter), the snail, the deer, the rabbits, the griffin, the cat,

and the dragon. The house rumbled a greeting.

Sam and Della stared. They looked at each other and smiled.

"Well," said Sam slowly. "I don't think we're going to be lonely after all, Della."

Chapter Six
Friends Forever

Neighbors say Sam and Della are queer people and that the house is full of strange noises. They say the garden is a jungle and that strange bonfires light up the cool evenings.